FOR BADGER K.H.

FOR FRIDA S.T.

First published 2016 by Walker Books Ltd
87 Vauxhall Walk, London SE11 5HJ

10 9 8 7 6 5 4 3 2 1

Text © 2016 Sean Taylor
Illustrations © 2016 Kate Hindley

The right of Sean Taylor and Kate Hindley to be identified as author
and illustrator respectively of this work has been asserted by them in
accordance with the Copyright, Designs and Patents Act 1988

This book has been typeset in ThrohandInk

Printed in China

All rights reserved. No part of this book may be reproduced, transmitted
or stored in an information retrieval system in any form or by any means,
graphic, electronic or mechanical, including photocopying, taping and
recording, without prior written permission from the publisher.

British Library Cataloguing in Publication Data: a catalogue record
for this book is available from the British Library

ISBN 978-1-4063-4560-5

www.walker.co.uk

WALKER BOOKS
AND SUBSIDIARIES

LONDON · BOSTON · SYDNEY · AUCKLAND

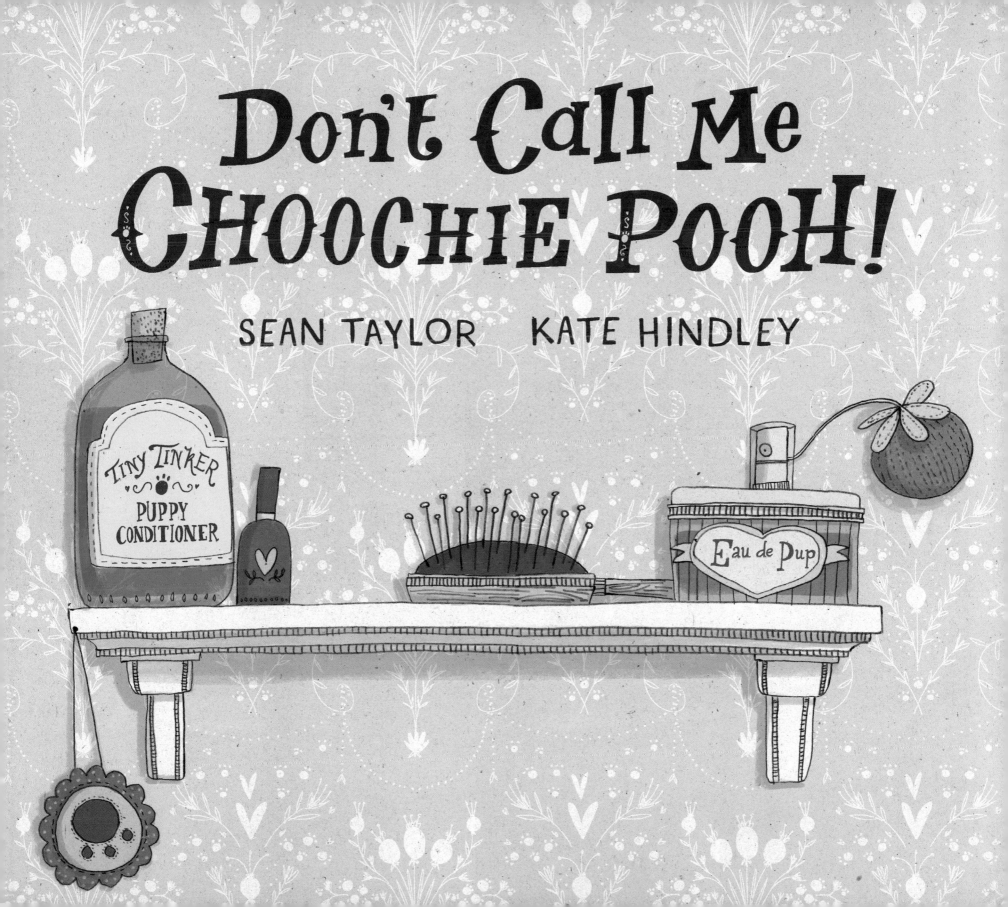

Don't Call Me CHOOCHIE POOH!

SEAN TAYLOR   KATE HINDLEY

I might be little,
but I'm not one of those
silly dogs you get.

I'm not frizzly...or fluffy...or daft. So, I don't know why my owner won't treat me like an ordinary, proper dog.

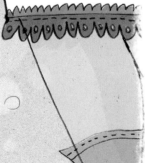

Because I'm little, my owner gives me heart-shaped Mini Puppy Treats.

They're the MOST embarrassing things you've ever seen.

CHOOCHIE

And last week we were walking down the street and she said to me,

COME ON, ICKLE PICKLE WOOF WOOF!

Did you know that other dogs can laugh
and make you feel very small? Well, they can.

Then, when she came out,
she picked me up and she KISSED me,
so everyone could see. And she said,
"Off we go, CHOOCHIE POOH!"

Be honest. Do I look like I should be called *THAT*?

I gave her an angry look as if to tell her,

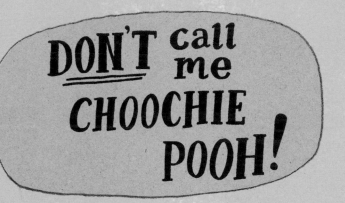

DON'T call me CHOOCHIE POOH!

But I don't think I'm good at angry looks because she said,

You're hungry, aren't you? LOOK, I've bought you some Mini Puppy Treats.

Then she put me
in her handbag!

What can you do?

AND CHIEF, WHO'S VERY BIG AND USED TO BE A POLICE DOG!

They were running about, barking, getting muddy and doing proper dog things.

Meanwhile I felt like a Mini-Puppy-Treat-eating-Choochie-Pooh in a handbag! And I thought they'd never ever want to play with me.

But I was wrong!
Because Chief looked at me
as if to say, "COME ON!"

So I did. And it was ...

BRILLIANT!

We played IT'S MY STICK!
(Where the main rule is you have
to growl as if you're really angry,
even though you're not.)

Then we played DOGS AND SAUSAGES!

(Which has complicated rules
that would take a long time to explain.)

And PUDDLE JUMPING!

(Which doesn't have any rules at all.)

I felt more over-excited than you can ever imagine.
It was like being a really proper dog!

What's more, Rusty, Bandit and Chief
all looked at me as if to say, "Come back
and play any time you want!"

THEN,
DISASTER STRUCK...

My owner called out,

Off we go OOPSIE BOOPSIE CHOOCHIE POOH!

I wanted to jump into a pit full of crocodiles.

I waited for my friends to laugh and make me feel very small. But actually ... Rusty's owner said,

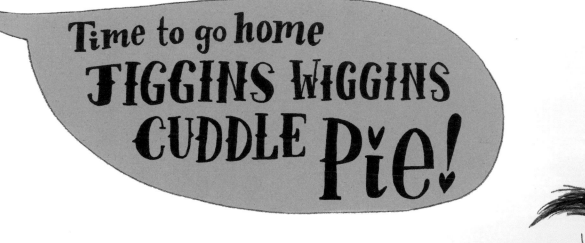

Time to go home TIGGINS WIGGINS CUDDLE Pie!

And Bandit's owner said,

come on, YOU LITTLE CUTIE PATOOTIE!

Then Chief's owner said,

Let's go HUNKY PUNKY PUMPKIN BOTTOM!

I looked at my new friends.

They looked at me.

We all looked at each other,
as if to say,

"What can you do?"

I play with them all the time now.

And I have to say that after all
the running and barking and
big dogs' games ...

even Mini Puppy Treats
taste quite good.